ME AND MY SISTER

A book to share from
Scallywag Press

FOR MY FAMILY

First published in Great Britain in 2019 by Scallywag Press Ltd,
10 Sutherland Row, London SW1V 4JT

This paperback edition published in 2020

Text and illustration copyright © 2019 by Rose Robbins

The rights of Rose Robbins to be identified as the author and illustrator of this work

have been asserted by her in accordance with the Copyright, Designs and Patents Act, 1988

All rights reserved

Art direction and design by Sarah Finan

Printed on FSC paper in Malaysia by Tien Wah Press

001

British Library Cataloguing in Publication Data available

ISBN 978-1-912650-23-1

ME AND MY SISTER

ROSE ROBBINS

Scallywag Press Ltd

LONDON

ME AND MY SISTER
LIKE DIFFERENT FOOD...

...BUT WE FINISH
AT THE SAME TIME.

MY SISTER LIKES TO WATCH TV BY HERSELF

SOMETIMES MY SISTER IS RUDE TO NANNA

BUT NANNA UNDERSTANDS

EVEN IF

I DON'T.

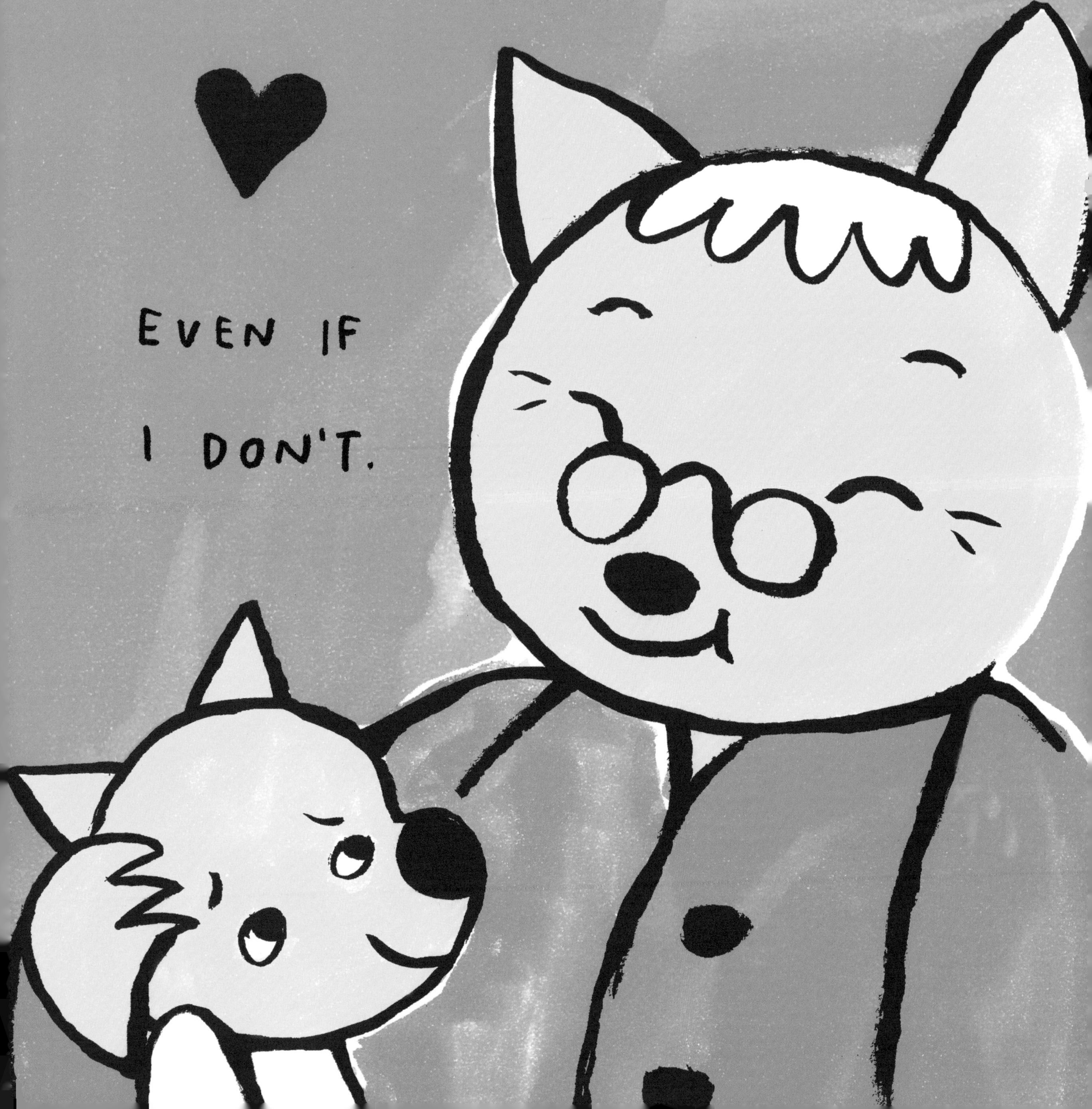

AND SOMETIMES SHE DOESN'T!

ME AND MY SISTER
GO TO DIFFERENT SCHOOLS.

WE DO DIFFERENT THINGS...

...AND WE BOTH LEARN A LOT!

AND MY SISTER DOESN'T.

MY SISTER
DOESN'T ALWAYS
LIKE HUGS

SO WE HIGH - FIVE INSTEAD!

ME AND MY SISTER

ARE VERY DIFFERENT...

BUT WE LOVE EACH OTHER JUST THE SAME.